Zip! Zoom! On a Broom

For the good witch in all my girls. —TS

For Dad. —RB

ISBN 978-1-338-32400-6

12 11 10 9 8 7 6 5 4 3 2   18 19 20 21 22 23

Printed in the U.S.A.   40

First Scholastic printing, October 2018

The illustrations of this book were made with India ink and watercolor on 300 lb Moulin du Roy hot pressed paper and finalized with Photoshop. The text was set in Providence Sans and the display type was hand-lettered by the illustrator. This book was edited by Mary-Kate Gaudet and designed by Kristina Iulo and Jen Keenan with art direction by Saho Fujii.

Zip! Zoom! On a Broom

Teri Sloat

Illustrated by
Rosalinde Bonnet

SCHOLASTIC INC.

One goes zip. **Two** go zoom.

Three witches glide from room to room.

Six haunt the basement down below.

Seven
chant.

Eight
incant.

Nine wicked witches rave and rant.

Ten take off, packed too tight.
Ten witches bicker, start to fight.

Ten witches push.

One shouts a curse,

"Broomstick,

zoomstick!

Hit reverse!"

Nine witches squabble, squirm for room.

One
topples
from the
plunging
broom.

YÉTI

Eight witches cast an ancient spell.

One witch goes POOF!

So long! Farewell!

Seven
spiral
through
a cloud.

One
witch
whirls
off,
shrieks
out
loud!

Six plummet down,
still holding on.

One gets zapped
by lightning—
gone!

Five witches drenched; they moan and groan.

One slides off, soaked to the bone.

One grip is slipping.

Four witches dripping in the sky.

Three upside down, still clinging tight.

One somersaults

into the night!

Two witches dropping to the ground.

One jumps off, lands safe and sound.

One witch yells her spell in time,

One witch glides across the moon.

Author and/or illustrator of over twenty-five picture books, TERI SLOAT has followed a path leading through teaching, bilingual education, and the arts. Her publishing career started in western Alaska and still calls her back to work with the strong oral tradition of folklore. This has led to a strong love of words and an exciting vocabulary. Other books by Teri include *There Was an Old Lady Who Swallowed a Trout* and *I'm a Duck!* Teri and her husband live in Northern California, where they enjoy grandchildren who tell their own stories.

As a kid, ROSALINDE BONNET loved to draw, write plays, and create sets for her puppets. So, after high school, she went to study art at the École Nationale Supérieure des Arts Décoratifs in Paris. Since her graduation, she has written and/or illustrated numerous children's books. She lives in Versailles, France.